I0602844

ANIMAL
TALES

Eyre Writers Inc

To find out more about Eyre Writers Inc
go to eyrewriters.com.au or
scan the QR code on the rear cover.

Editors: Aileen Pluker and Helen van Rooijen
Technical Wizards:
Diane Hester, Mary Gudzenovs

Paperback ISBN: 978-0-6488970-4-0
eBook ISBN: 978-0-6488970-5-7

CONTENTS

The Dog Who Climbed Trees

Barkley was the ugliest dog I have ever seen. Even as a pup the texture and colour of his coat looked more like the product of a collision between his parents than a mating.

He seemed to be made up of discarded parts. A tail that went off at right angles halfway along, ears much too hig for his head, flopping over his face, and stumpy legs with huge paws and claws that gave more than a hint of prehistoric genes present in his makeup.

He was a natural in the paddock. Sheep fell into regimented lines and marched into the sheep yards needing little more than a reminder nip to the legs and a warning yap when Barkley was on the Job. And the cattle certainly thought twice about making a break for the mulga if he was around.

His temperament and co-ordination were those of a happy drunk and this, combined with his appearance, was enough to ensure unwanted visitors to the farm stayed in their cars. The fact that he had a habit of jumping up on the bonnet and barking his welcome through the windscreen didn't help their peace of mind either.

It was probably this habit of scrambling up on vehicles that enabled him to expand his climbing skills to trees, that and an overwhelming desire to 'fetch' again and again and again whatever anyone threw his way.

Our neighbour, Freddy Lawson, was probably the one who started Barkley on his tree-climbing career. Old Freddy called in one day to borrow windmill buckets, and as usual the dog presented him with the inevitable stick to be thrown.

For a while Fred obliged but soon tired of the game and although it might have been his intention to ignore the dog, Barkley had other ideas.

He never accepted rejection. His idea was if you persevered and gave out enough hints like pushing the stick between the thrower's legs time and time again, the thrower would relent and chuck it just once more.

Freddy was heard to mumble something about Barkley's parentage and grabbed the stick for the umpteenth time. He made as if to throw it along the track then turned and tossed it into the nearest mallee tree. It landed in the boughs about twelve feet from the ground. He grinned.

'See if you can get that, you ugly little bugger.'

And Barkley did! Straight up the tree, claws digging into the gnarled wood, tail manoeuvring like a tightrope-walker's pole and a single-mindedness that precluded any possibility of failure. He grabbed the stick and did a wobbly one eighty.

With the grace of an arthritic, three-legged cat he managed to reach the ground, the stick still held firmly in his mouth.

He trotted across to Fred, dropped the prize at his feet and sat back, eyes flicking from Fred's face to the stick.

'Well I'll be damned,' Freddy Lawson said.

That was twelve years ago.

Barkley still climbs trees but not as high. He's outside now, up the Lilly Pilly – asleep with the cat.

Kathy Blacker

Burn-Outs In The Sky

These country roads are lined with trees
sheltered channels of gentle breeze
corrugated, limestone-riddled
pot-holed, boggy, rarely driven

So why is it every six a.m. walk
I'm forced to side-step, shuffle and balk
traffic rushing me thick and fast
rush hour in some city vast

Not with cars do I share the way
not with semis, trucks or drays,
not even stock or a plague of rabbits
but a bloody great mob of lunatic parrots

P-platers testing their skill at the wheel
forcing tyres to screech and squeal
swerving, swooping, doubling back
at speeds that would trip any radar trap

They appear as tiny specks in the distance
floating head-high above the road surface
three or four at a time join the spree
flying toward me with manic glee

meters only before my face
they part to begrudge me my bit of space
wing tips brush the side of my cheek
a lone pink feather floats to my feet

With all the acres on either side
and the freedom to fly clear up to the sky
why do these aerial hoons persist
in fighting me for this one little stretch?

Is this road any safer, does it lead somewhere special?
Do they find here an up-draft beyond all measure?
Is it just to be feisty or mean that they come?
Or is it, simply ... just to have fun.

Diane Hester

Family Ties

'Fancy meeting you here,' he smiled at me. He held the wide grin of my youth, but his eyes tugged at each corner now.

'We have a habit of meeting in the unlikeliest of places,' I joked, walking in and relaxing into the chair next to him. 'Remember that pub in Dublin?'

He brown eyes sparkled from the memory.

'You didn't have to come back you know,' he scolded. His voice was soft, but the room hung heavy with the meaning.

'Of course I did,' I replied. 'You'd have done the same for me.'

Our eyes locked.

'Absolutely,' he agreed.

#

'You can't save it, Ness,' he was stroking along the poor beast's course woollen back. 'She's too far gone. The kindest thing would be to put her out of her misery.'

'Rubbish!' I replied, putting on my most determined mask and clenching my teeth. 'She just needs a leg splint, that's all. '

I bent over the forlorn body and found a couple of ill-formed sticks. 'Help and find me something to bind these with.'

He reached down and took off his gumboots and socks. He passed them over to me.

'These do?'

'I'll give it my best,' I said, my tongue poking out the side as I tied his socks tight around the lamb's leg and the wood.

#

'So are they treating you okay in here?' I asked, reaching over to pour him water from the seventies style carafe. Its edges were rough and jaded. He groaned, pushing himself higher in the bed.

'Can't complain,' his face took on a grey hue. 'Sick of the bloody needles though.'

'Fair enough,' I replied. The smell of disinfectant hung between us.

#

The sharp tang of stale piles of wool and dung clung to the air. Above us the old wooden shed creaked and groaned like a ship's hull, as the wind howled through its bare bones.

'You need to chase them into the shoot, so I can drench them,' he informed me. 'Like this.'

He waved his arms frantically, like a hummingbird about to crash.

The sheep stood for a moment and stared at him, their dull eyes not even blinking. With a clatter, the lead ewe took off across the trampled dirt floor towards the shoot.

'Yah! Yah!' he cried at them.

But the cunning old girl stopped just short of the entrance, dug her toes in and turned like a ballerina doing a pirouette. She bashed into the fence at the side with the other sheep barrelling behind her.

'Watch out! 'I cried, my heart thumping hard in my chest.

#

'I heard the guys have brought you a Holden.' I sat listening to the blip of the monitor. Its rhythmic beeping was comforting.

'Yeah,' he laughed, the effort causing him to wince. 'They want to go on a tiki tour of Aotearoa when I am allowed out of here.'

'Cool,' I looked out of the window and up at the blue sky. 'Sounds like fun. Do you know when?'

'Dunno,' he sighed. 'Soon I hope. I need to get outta here.'

#

'So are you coming to stay this school holidays?' he asked, his voice sounding deeper on the phone than I remembered from last time.

'Dunno. Depends what Nanna says.' I twirled the cord around my finger. 'I think so.'

'Cool,' he said. 'I've got some more wool sacks.'

'OK. But you know my Mum gets a bit funny about us hill sliding. She reckons I'm going to break something one day.'

'Nah,' he assured me. 'We've been doing it for years. It's safe as.'

#

I didn't have long left before I needed to be back at work. Days, maybe a couple of weeks.

'I'll have to fly back soon,' I said, as much to myself as him. I wasn't able to look him in the eye. 'But there's no rush really.'

'Maybe you can come with us on tour?' he said, his gaze followed mine out of the window.

'It's just me and the boys, but I don't think they'll mind.'

I considered it but only for a moment. 'I've got to get back to London. Job and all that.'

'Yeah,' he said, his voice holding a small wobble. 'No worries. I get it mate.'

A silence fell on the room.

#

He broke through the silent stalemate.

'Why are you wearing makeup?' his voice was tight and angry. 'You never used to be into girly shit like that. '

'I dunno.' I clenched my teeth. We had been arguing all morning. 'Cos I want to.'

'Whatever,' he replied, turning his back on me. I hated to fight with him.

'So what did you want to do this afternoon?' I asked. 'Maybe we could take the four wheelers and go for a spin?'

He paused, his taught back still facing me.

"Nah,' he grunted. 'I better get back to the house. Dad will probably want a hand rounding up the sheep for shearing. '

'I can help,' I offered.

'Nah don't worry about it,' he said, sad eyes turning back to face me. 'You'll just ruin your makeup.'

#

'Well I guess I'd better head off. I can come back tomorrow.' I tried to make a note of every freckle on his face. They were darker than usual against his pale skin.

'Yeah,' a small tear clung to the edge of his eye.

'I wish there was something else I could do to help.' I reached forward to pull him into a hug.

His body tensed and he let out a small grunt.

'Oh sorry,' I said, releasing him carefully back into the pillows. 'Did that hurt?'

'Nah,' he grimaced, his mouth a solid line. 'They are coming back to put stem cells into my spine later on. That's going to hurt.'

'Shit.' My hands trembled and I couldn't stop them. 'God. I'm so sorry.'

'I'll be fine.' He held onto my hand for a moment longer. 'I'm not ready to go just yet.' He gave it a small squeeze.

I paused for a moment.

'Yeah me neither.' I sat back down again. 'I can wait with you.'

'Cheers.' The room fell silent. We both looked outside at the blue flash of the sky.

'Would have been a great day for a hill slide,' he said.

'Sure would have,'' I replied.

VK Tritschler

Like Ella

(Ella Fitzgerald 1918-1996)

Dawn –

a pale sun slips above the horizon,
has almost caught the quarter moon
and mists holding the night.

Foggy tentacles shroud the trees,
tether damp hills and still waters.
Lone magpie on a stark branch stage

fills its throat and,
like Ella, scats a melody down
the waiting valley – into memory.

'How high the moon'

Helen van Rooijen

Andreas and the Donkey

'It's bloody cold in the rooms,' Ray informed them, backing up to the fire and rubbing his hands. 'I'm gunna drag me mattress in here and sleep on the floor.'

'Good idea,' Jamie agreed. 'I think I'll do the same.'

'You Australians. So weak. Call this cold? Why I remember one night in Crete.'

I grinned, got another tinnie from the Eski, topped up Andraes' drink and settled back. Andraes always told the best yarns.

He had only been a kid when the Germans parachuted into Crete. They thought it would be a walkover but they reckoned without the Cretans. The British garrison was suddenly supplemented by the heroic resistance of the Cretan population, old men, young boys and women, with any weapon they could find. Of course it was an unequal battle, but those ten days saw some of the fiercest fighting of the war. Although most of the Allied forces were either evacuated or captured, quite a number were stranded in the mountains or in villages and, with many of the local fighters, took to the hills to continue the fight. Together they formed a resistance movement whose job it was to harry the Germans and report enemy movements. Like many other red blooded Cretans, Andraes became part of this group.

Looking at him today, well into middle age, arguably too old for the tough life of a shearer, you can still see the strength in his wiry body and work worn hands, catch a little of the fire in his bright, brown eyes. He still has a full head of wiry, black hair and fierce barbwire eyebrows. What a sight he must have been at 15, running over rough roads, hiding in rocky crevasses, carrying heavy loads and guiding men to safety. Yes, it was worth staying up to listen to one of Andraes' stories because they were all true.

He took a mouthful of the rotgut he drank, let the fiery liquid run down his throat, let out a contented sigh and began.

'It would have been about October of the second year, not yet real winter, more days and days of howling winds and icy rain, that I got a call to take a new transmitter to Captain Johnston. He was holed up in a small cave just outside the town of Drakona. I knew the area well. Some of my relatives came from those parts. It was not so far from Suda Bay where the submarine had landed some food supplies along with the transmitter, but it was quite mountainous and there were German patrols in the area.

The Colonel loaned me a donkey to carry the load. All life is hard in Crete, but the hardest life of all is that of a donkey. He is loaded down until he almost sinks to the ground, then he must carry that load along rocky tracks, up and down hills and over mountain passes: no one would ever wish to come back in another life as a donkey.

Well this donkey was old, but he was willing. We loaded the transmitter on one side and about 20 okas of wheat on the other. It was smooth going for a while, smooth but slow. This donkey was no racehorse. But when the track began to rise he became slower and slow-er. I had expected to make the journey in four hours, but we were already six hours on the road and still a long way from our destination.

So I did a foolish thing. I decided to take the direct route through the village of Kanarus. The route was shorter and the grading was easier. I did it for the sake of the donkey, but was he grateful? No he was not. He went slower and slower, one foot, two foot and all the while puffing and blowing. If he had used as much energy walking as he did in huffing and puffing we would have been through the village in no time.

I was almost reaching the end of the village when – no! Ahead of me were two German soldiers ,and, of course that stupid donkey took that exact moment to let out a mournful bray.

The soldiers looked around and pointed at us. I gave the beast a prod with my stick to hurry it up, but would it go any faster? No. If anything it went even slower, any more and it would have been standing still.

The soldier walked towards me. 'Slow donkey,' one of them said, in poor Greek.

'Plenty stick,' said the other.

'Plenty stick, no food, donkey done for.' I informed them, hoping they would be satisfied. But no.

'No. Not done for, lazy,' and, with that, one of the soldiers picked up a large stick and gave the poor animal a tremendous whack. The poor thing was so surprised he took three running steps then stood stock still, protesting to the skies.

'Come, come, more stick,' said the other and began beating my poor animal also.

The donkey tried, if only to get away from his tormentors but he was too old and the load too heavy. He would trot a few paces then stop and they would run after him, laughing and whacking.

Part of me was outraged at their treatment of my animal, but the rest of me was mortally afraid that the beast would collapse and the contents of the load would be discovered. I dragged and dragged at the rope around his neck trying to get him away from the soldiers, while judging how far I would have to run before I reached the safety of the mountains, if the worst happened.

Just when I was sure disaster was upon me, three village girls came to my rescue.

Attracted by the donkey's brays and the antics of the Germans they began pointing and laughing. Soldiers all over the world are the same. Who wants to meddle with a peasant boy and his donkey when there are pretty girls around? The soldiers turned from me and ambled over to the girls and began flirting.

Relieved, I tried to move the beast as quickly as possible and the poor thing, wanting to get away from his tormenters, was as anxious as I was to leave that village. I turned up the first side road I came to.

Andraes stopped his narrative and leaned forward, gazing into the fire. 'Yes, for sure, I was a lucky boy that day.'

'Great story,' Jamie said. 'but what's it got to do with being cold?'

'Oh that, that happened later, after I had delivered the transmitter. Now that's another story.' And he reached out to refill his glass.

Aileen Pluker

Swan

Over the shallow bars

between sea and shore

a swan

drifts through the spaces

between night and morning.

Her uncrowned head, poised on a lily stem,

curves down to her inversion,

and poses a question, marked

in silhouette

against an underwater sunrise.

Alison Manthorpe

Jim and Mr Peter

On the third morning of the early spring storm old Jim's body was found on the beach. When, the day before, Mr Peter's corpse and the splintered woods of their clinker built dinghy were thrown up by the sea, the police and the shack people knew old Jim must be gone too.

His neighbours sat with Jim quietly waiting until the police had looked, probed, and taken their photos, and the coroner's van came to take him away for the necessary government final reckoning of his life. Then they would get him back to bury him, with his friend, in the little bush cemetery near the shack town.

People knew Jim well, for it seemed like forever since he and his old mother had arrived and had settled into the coastal-dune holiday shack community. She cared possessively for her simple natured, man-child son and most people had forgotten her name if it were ever first given. One day however, she was taken off to hospital after a 'wee turn', and died within the week. Jim just stayed on looking after himself in his tiny hut, overflowing with beach-combing treasures.

The years rolled on. Jim, clad in an odd assortment of found clothing and woolen hats, played with the children on the summer beach. He taught many to fish with hand lines and to whittle driftwood. Twisting up his face, Jim would make the bird calls, seeming to communicate with his feathered friends with ease. He was trusted as the friend of the children over the years and he never betrayed that trust.

When the community built wooden swings for the children, Jim put seaweed and sand under them to soften the ground against the children's falls. 'Come on', he'd shout to the children, 'You can swing now. It's safe now.' And they did. Taking his laughing turn on the swings he was pushed by the children and walked all wobbly when he got off.

Jim patrolled the line of shacks after storms tidying debris, and, delighted by the shape of beach stones, he collected thousands and edged the pathways between the shacks with them. He was given a pot of white paint and the shack area took on an ordered and festive look after he painted the stones. He fished from his little boat on calm days and shared the fish he caught. People brought an extra loaf of fresh bread, some fruit or a chocolate bar for him when they went to town shopping.

Then Mr Peter arrived. He appeared one day at Jim's side and was proudly introduced as his friend. The shabby, be-whiskered pair were always together, sharing everything and Mr Peter sat in the bow of the little boat when old Jim fished. They ate a simple diet of fish, bread and tomatoes, potatoes and cabbages from their garden. It was all they needed, but when there was a summer barbecue anywhere along the line of shacks they were expected. 'Come on Mr Peter. We are going to have sausages', old Jim would call, and they would attend. They both loved ice cream and smacked their lips savoring the taste.

One autumn evening Mr Peter appeared, very distressed, at a neighbor's shack. They went home with him to find old Jim had fallen breaking his hip. He was taken to hospital where it was discovered Jim had no income and no Medicare number. He didn't exist in records and he was not even sure of the spelling of his name. The hospital social workers, after righting these wrongs, were concerned about him coping when he got home –

and so the problems started.

The officials were shocked to find there was no electricity connected to the shack; candles for light, and cooking over open fires - 'so dangerous considering.' As they were not told that the old friends often slept in their 'outside lounge', on worn chairs and an old settee, with the sky, sheoaks and gum trees as their ceiling, their sensibilities thus were not further outraged. However the well-meaning bureaucracy had the opinion that 'something had to be done.'

Old Jim recovered, and with Mr Peter, continued on seemingly immune to the halo of perceived problems around them. They limped their gray haired way around the shack area, with Jim using a splendid dolphin handled walking stick he had carved himself. Mr Peter's legs were somewhat shaky but they covered the distances they had always walked. The garden beds were dug ready for planting tomato seeds on the first warm spring days, when the government cars returned.

The words were kind, reasonable by any standards, and final. Jim and Mr Peter could not stay safely where they were and must move immediately to a 'lovely little unit' in the town. Old Jim listened and both nodded with apparent comprehension. Their neighbors argued, divided as to what was best, and in the end the officials in their government cars went away to make the arrangements.

That night the storms started; the winds rattled the shacks and huge waves swept high up the beach. In the morning old Jim and Mr Peter took their little boat and went to sea.

There was no doubt the shack community would bury their friends and share all costs, however the undertaker would not bury them together. 'It would not be seemly, nor perhaps legal,' he insisted. He could not bury an old man and his old cat in one coffin and one grave no matter the depth of their friendship. The police arrived when tempers began to fray. Taking the city undertaker to one side they spoke persuasively to him, for they had felt the community's love and grieving reaction to the deaths of their own.

Two days later the final ceremony in the sun-dappled bush cemetery was enacted. The shack people stood together and each gently placed a white painted beach stone around the simple grave with the driftwood notice:

JIM AND MR PETER
FRIENDS FOREVER TOGETHER

Helen van Rooijen

The Cat's Choice

With a nonchalant air I adorn the new chair
That's supposed to belong to my human,
It's a Jason recliner, for a cat there's no finer
But for both there is too little room in!

Once settled in place, it's a thorough disgrace
When my human removes me elsewhere
To a moth-eaten mat that's no place for a cat
So much for that comfortable chair!

If he's going to do that to his poor bloody cat
I don't want to be part of this household,
I shall pack up and leave for I know he won't grieve
If I live in a second-hand mouse-hole!

So in protest I voice my alternative choice
To depart from this miserable scene,
It's too bad he's like that, so damn mean to his cat,
Oh to think how my life could have been!

Adrian McFarlane

Haunting Sound of Bagpipes

Another patch of fog loomed and then vanished before the moving vehicle.

Carolyn shuddered. She didn't like it. It was too fragile. Carolyn liked things to be solid. Real. They were easier to deal with that way.

The ghost stories the locals at the pub had told in front of the fire didn't help. Not that she believed in ghosts, but the atmosphere out here was conducive to odd thoughts. The fog muffled any sound, so Carolyn was surrounded by silence – except for the crunch of teeth on bone.

Dandelion, her best friend's Highland Terrier was oblivious to Carolyn's concerns as he polished off the T-Bone she had salvaged from her evening meal.

'Do you have to make so much noise?' Carolyn complained, but she didn't really mind. The radio didn't work in Amy's car and she felt that total silence might have been a bit too much.

She was starting to regret having offered to take Dandelion into town for his annual checkup. Amy was laid up with the flu and didn't want the terrier to miss his appointment.

At least the heaters worked in the old car. That was some comfort.

Carolyn's mind wandered back irresistibly to the tales of the old men. One story in particular seemed to stick in her mind. Probably because the legend was centred on the area she was now travelling through.

Mackenzie Brockman – that was his name – a piper, who had fallen from the ruined tower of the castle, while playing the bagpipes. The castle was subsequently closed to the public until it could be made safe. When it was reopened, visitors to the castle had reported being guided by a man carrying a set of bagpipes and had later identified him as Mackenzie Brockman.

The castle was now a popular tourist destination as people flocked to see if they could meet the dead piper.

Carolyn had passed the castle a few miles back and was only five or six miles from Amy's cottage when Dandelion gave a strangled choke from the rear seat.

Glancing over her shoulder Carolyn couldn't see in the dark what was wrong, but the choking sound continued. She braked hard and slid to a stop in the middle of the narrow bitumen road.

'Dandy! What have you done?' Panic raced through her system. Amy was devoted to that dog.

Jumping out, she wrenched open the back door, engine still running and the headlights lighting up the road ahead. It vaguely occurred to her that it was strange that she hadn't seen the hitchhiker until he asked if everything was OK.

'The dog's choking!' she called, hauling the convulsing bundle of white fur from the back seat and into the beams in front of the car.

The man dumped his bundle on the verge and knelt beside the pair.

'The bone's stuck in his teeth and some of it's blocking his throat. Hold his head still,' the stranger instructed.

Carolyn did as she was told, concern for the dog and a certain amount of guilt for giving him the bone in the first place, claiming her attention. In ordinary circumstances she would have been wary of the stranger.

His accent was thick but she could still understand him. The month she had spent here so far had sharpened her understanding of the various levels of accented speech.

He was about forty she guessed, with a kind face and large gentle hands. She watched anxiously as he worked the bone from between the dog's teeth.

Dandy coughed and spluttered, trying to shake his head but was restricted by Carolyn's firm grip.

'There you go little man,' he crooned, dropping the bone and checking the dog's mouth for any other stray pieces, 'All done.'

Carolyn released him and the dog shook himself vigorously from head to tail. He then took a good look at the stranger, growled, backed away and commenced barking hysterically.

'Dandy! You ungrateful little sod! Get back in the car,' Carolyn scolded, embarrassed by the dogs behaviour. Dandy bolted into the back seat and curled up in the far corner, shivering.

Carolyn slammed the car door.

'Sorry about that, I dunno what's gotten into him, he's my friend Amy's dog, he's usually so friendly. Thank you for helping, I'm not that good with animals myself.'

The man smiled and nodded.

'Can I give you a lift somewhere?' she asked, feeling honour-bound to return his kindness.

He shook his head and smiled again.

'Nay, I live around here.' He stooped to pick up his bundle from the verge.

'What's your name? I'm sure Amy would like to come and thank you herself – she lives just up the road a few miles.'

When he turned back to face her she noticed the bundle had

sticks poking out of it.

A set of bagpipes.

He answered her before the thought had even fully formed in her mind,

'My name is Mackenzie Brockman miss. It was very nice to meet you and your wee doggy.'

Carolyn gaped. It couldn't be the same Mackenzie Brockman – but then, Dandy had reacted so strangely to him. She had heard about animals being sensitive to ghosts.

She shook her head and laughed. 'You're joking right? He's dead!'

The man nodded in agreement.

'Five years gone. Drive careful miss,' he added – and vanished like the mist from before her eyes.

Carolyn stood and stared at the spot where he had been, heart pounding. She was shocked, but not frightened, which amazed her even more. She had spoken – actually spoken – to a dead man.

She smiled. She could imagine the faces of the old men when she told them.

'Goodnight Mackenzie Brockman, it was nice to meet you too,' she whispered.

As if in response, the air around her began to vibrate with sound which gradually transformed into the opening notes of Amazing Grace.

Carolyn listened in respectful silence. The 'haunting sound of bagpipes' would never have the same meaning for her again.

Mary Gudzenovs

Cat

Our old cat died last week. At 17 plus she had run her race and simply faded away.

There is no question of ownership, although we called her ours, and in the way of the best of cats we didn't own her – we belonged to her.

Puss was a beautiful creature, a long-haired tabby with exquisite markings and large splashes of white. She could hold her place in any beauty ranks and well she knew it.

As with all our previous cats she came unannounced. Given to us with a gruff, 'Found her on my place. Was going to shoot her as a stray, then thought you were soft enough to give her a home'. She was already just past the kitten stage and had been desexed – still had the blue stitches in her side. We did the usual; contacted the vets and put an ad in the paper. No one knew her or claimed her and after a hassle when I removed the sutures, she moved in.

Family life was never the same. The boys, rowdy and clumsy preteens, became enlisted as her willing allies. House rules were demolished as she commanded sleeping spots on the ends of beds, sunny areas wherever she chose and was always in the way. She was adept at pretending it was too cold to be put out at night and stayed by the fire with her 'poor cat look' and a very satisfied purr. Puss draped over chairs and windowsills contemplating universal questions, or sleeping... it was hard to tell the difference. She never explained her actions as no aristocratic cat ever does.

She plonked herself into the middle of any game or paper

spread on the floor, rearranged war games pieces, chessmen, knitting and pencils. Puss kept her contract as a mousecatcher par excellence but twice she brought live mice into the house to present to us, then dropped them. Result – we were the ones chasing mice for days!

She was belled for chasing birds. Usually, with us, her manners were perfection itself with conversational 'please', and 'thank-you' in mews and purrs. She could admonish when she felt it necessary. Once she gently bit a friend of the boys, who had, obviously in her opinion, behaved with less than gentlemanly manner with her. They remained friends. and he was most contrite. With us, if we displeased her, like coming home from an obvious fishing trip with no fish for her, or any other misdemeanor, she would give us 'the back'. Sometimes, in cat fashion we would get 'the back' just because she needed, at that moment, to reaffirm that she was a cat and not a fawning dog, thank you!

With other animals Puss was not a lady and her manners lacked a certain classiness. Other cats – except an elderly one eyed neighbour cat with whom she would share sleeping spots on the roof on lazy autumn mornings – and dogs were dispatched out of the yard in a fury. If the offending animal were not speedy enough it would be put right out of the street. Puss would return, hissing dark comments about the trespasser and demand to go onto the balcony where she could oversee her domain again.

Grooming was meticulous on those occasions.

When Puss was 15 years of age we moved house to a five-acre lot with a very extended horizon. She was now quite deaf and slow and we worried about her ability to adjust. What a laugh! After days of spookiness, when she scuttled from furniture to door to deck, she found her comfort zone and conquered the new property. A pert youthfulness was regained and she oversighted the work to be done, sitting with dignity just where rocks were to be moved, perched on the completed fish pond walls, attended barbecues, and demanded her usual attention from us and any guests. The birds soon learned that she was harmless and teased her. We never witnessed how she coped initially with the electric fence that kept the cattle steers in the paddock but she always lowered her tail when she went under the wires.

Whenever we went out she followed, calling and conversing loudly – a noisy demanding shadow.

Last weekend Puss attended her last function; and then when all the family had sat with her, stroked and petted her, and said 'Goodbye' she was gone. She now has a secluded final place, with a view, and the morning sun. A new tree has been planted near to commemorate her life and give her shelter when the days become hot or too cold.

Puss was present at most of the rights of passage for us all during her long life. We played together, laughed with and at her, celebrated graduations together, and we cried tears into her fur in the bad times. She was there to gently stroke when we were reflective or stressed. Of course we loved her, in fact were quite dotty about her. Will we be crass enough to want another cat after her? Naturally - yes we will. The relationship was so good that we will be delighted, in time, when another cat chooses us, elicits our love, and rearranges our lives to suit herself.

Next time we may even agree on a name...

Helen van Rooijen

From the Farm Gate

Egg-pinching crows sit on the chook yard fence
waiting
kookaburras
down by the shearing shed
burst into manic laughter
inviting me to join in
why not?
no one will hear

a shadow blinks across my eyes
wedgie and his mate
in lazy loops
scroll over a pad of grey
finger-tipped wings
sadly
inscribing their requiem

the wind
like some mischievous frosty imp
tickling my legs with an icy touch
steals any warmth from a watery sun

I see the slaughter tree
tomorrow's roast hangs in reverent anticipation
of the coming baptism of mint sauce and rosemary

the cattle bless 'em
smoke at both ends in the frosty air
blissfully ignorant of their place in nature's
meltdown
the forever cycle
in one end
out the other

Kathy Blacker

Brolga Boy

An antiquated aircraft sat on the tarmac at the remote Edward River Aboriginal community in Far North Queensland. With a crew of three and myself the only passenger, it rattled along the costal airstrip and lumbered into the air.

Sea birds scattered, disturbed by the noisy man-made version. Away in the distance thousands of black and white magpie geese rose from a large lagoon.

Whirling in unison, wings beating forcibly, they gained height, turned in one beautiful choreographed, anticlockwise movement and escaped inland, away from the path of the intruder.

The aircraft began its descent, sweeping low over the wide river estuary and touched down on the gravelly Aurukun airstrip. All was quiet, trees almost motionless in the gentle breeze that barely cooled my sweaty forehead.

The view ahead towards the community was unremarkable except for that of a small hoy doing some sort of jig beside the track.

He was skinny, bare-chested and wearing a pair of frayed, too large shorts, that appeared to defy the laws of gravity staying on his bony hips as he continued his dance. I guessed his age at about eleven – or twelve. He did not seem to notice me as I walked towards him.

The intrinsic movements of his dance were breath-taking. Staccato foot stomping blended into graceful fluid movements as he crouched low, stooping forward with outstretched hands brushing the grass stems, reminding me of a large bird browsing.

In time these calm movements gave way to energetic leaping.

Jumping high he raised his thin, bony arms, spread them first outward then above his head, finishing with a sharp, clapping of his hands. This seemingly insignificant action was further highlighted as he tilted his head backwards, challenging the sky, his wide mouth open.

Under my unbelieving gaze his human form diminished. He became a Brolga in all of its form and spirit. Arms became wings and gaping mouth, a sky-reaching, open beak of the bird.

The boy now in the spiritual form of an adult bird danced the Brolga mating dance, emulating the bird's choreography to the finest detail. He was now the Brolga. Then, as if no further magic was possible, the patch of trembling grass behind the boy opened and I could see a Brolga chick attempting to copy the boy's movements as he demonstrated to the blrd the mating dance of its parent.

I could keep my quiet no longer and gasped loudly in amazement at what I was both seeing and imagining. How could this young Aboriginal boy display movements so realistically, capturing spiritually the essence of the bird?

The boy stopped his dance and turned to see who had caused the interruption. I begged him to continue but he smiled.

'It is alright. I have finished now. My little bird is tired. He is learning, very well, to be a Brolga.'

'How do you know this dance?' I asked in astonishment. 'And why are you teaching the little chick?'

'I am his Daddy and it is my job to teach him to dance,' he replied solemnly.

'But why are you his daddy and how are you able to do this?'

I asked.

'I am an Aboriginal boy and we know these things. I found this little bird in the bush after his Mummy and Daddy had died so he is my responsibility. That is why I am teaching him.'

He said this as if it was the most natural of responses. I could not think of another question. The boy's answers had been so complete and simple.

'Are you walking to Aurukun?' he asked.

'Yes. I think the Councillor has forgotten me but that's fine. I can walk. Shall we walk together?'

The chick jumped and launched itself into the boy's arms. He quickly took hold of the bird, tucking it under his left arm and offered his free hand to mine.

To this day I recall vividly the feel of his bony hand in mine as we walked towards the Shire Office, discussing the spiritual beings of animals, birds and people. I embraced a new world, the world of the Aboriginal people.

It became a world of enlightenment, in part hindered by an in-between universe as I attempted to blend my new reality with the pragmatism of my daily routine. Something that would continue to interrupt my new reality with the pragmatism of my western beliefs for years to come.

I ceased my inner thoughts and turned my attention to the boy who had continued his chatter as I had drifted off.

He told me how he liked learning new things at the small school at Aurukun but also learning from the stories told to him by his father and uncles about the past times of his ancestors. He said he felt good when speaking his own Wik language and learning about ancient times.

Our stroll along the track ended far too soon. On arrival the president of the shire approached with outstretched hand.

'Good morning,' he said. 'I see you have already met the young Keeper of our traditions.'

'I've had a wonderful time watching this young man performing the Brolga mating dance and his bonding with the little bird,' I told him. 'I was amazed that it embraced him with such trust.'

He smiled. 'I am so pleased that you appreciate the skills of our people. Now the least we can do is invite you to our Christmas lunch we have planned for this afternoon.'

'Thank you. I would like to join you all for lunch but I have already received the greatest Christmas gift I will ever be given. I have seen a boy become a brolga before my very eyes. I am only sad that I might never see it again.'

The President smiled.

Lee Clayton

The Sheep Farmer's Daughter

She ran with her sisters and brother,
between the gums and sheoaks,
to meet the school bus.
Tried so hard at ballet,
excelled at art.
Loved her horses, the sheep
And the farm dogs.
Enjoyed the beach,
and picnics in the scrub.
Lunch with Dad up the paddock.
Cooking and sewing with Mum.
Time spent with grandma and granny.
Then she moved on to Uni and new friends,
far away with a man we hardly knew.
We missed that glorious smile.
Working on the airlines,
she flew across Australia
and travelled overseas.
She explored wonderful new places
that we will never see.
Love of art took her to the Louvre
and galleries across Europe.
Through the years she brought friends home,
to show them her old haunts.
Always with that smile.
How we wished she would stay a while.
We cherished the calls and visits,

and then she brought her children home.
A new generation to share her smiles,
her tears and laughter through those precious years.
Her smile will never leave us,
but now our tears run like water
for our beautiful sheep farmer's daughter.

Ross Hudson

Vigil

Will Parker had led a hard life. In his time he'd been navy, roustabout, sheerer, well-digger, farmer's labourer and any other job that came to hand. He was old, gnarled and grey, like an old gum tree that had existed on too little water for a long time.

There was still life in him, but not much.

Years ago he had been tall and handsome, in a rugged fashion. He had been quite a man with the ladies and had sired two or three kids during his travels. He had even acquired a wife along the way. That had been a mistake for both of them. He could hardly remember her name now.

But, all through his life he had had one constant companion, a dog. 'A man can't be all bad if a dog loves him' he used to joke. He had had several dogs over the years, some died of old age, others died from snakebite or accidents, but his best dog, his best mate, was Nugget, a black and white bitza. Nugget's mother must have had morals rather like his own to have produced an animal with such a varied pedigree.

Will had had Nugget since he was a pup, hardly old enough to drink by himself. He had lived in the pocket of Will's old coat until he was old enough to keep up with his master as he tramped the weary miles between there and the next place.

Now they were both old and slow. It was going to be a toss-up which of them would go first. The way he was feeling, Will thought it might be him. He wasn't worried about dying but he didn't want to spend days lying useless in the bush unable to help himself. He was also worried about what would happen to

Nugget when he went.

Neither of them was capable of the long treks of yore. They had to stay close to civilization where towns were no more than two or three day's supply apart. On a good day they could make ten to fifteen miles, but at the end, they would be exhausted. Will collapsing by the side of the road, desperately trying to summon the energy to make camp, and Nugget lying, panting, his head on Will's knee.

'I think it's all up with me mate,' Will confided to Nugget, patting the old, salt and pepper head. 'What say, tomorrow we struggle into town and I try to find a quack? He might be able to give me a pill to keep me goin'. I'm also goin' to see if I can find someone who'll look after you. I'm gettin' beyond it, mate, you know that. But I'm not goin' to leave you with anyone. I'll see you right mate, don't you worry. What do you think?'

Will slept fitfully throughout the night, often listening to his heart to make sure it hadn't betrayed him and testing his lungs to see if they would inflate. He had a pain somewhere in his chest. He could ignore it through the day, but during the long hours between sunset and sunrise it would torment him, playing on his fears.

'Must be gettin' soft or somethin',' he muttered to himself.

Nugget too, was restive, snuggling closer as if to gain warmth and strength from the one being who was his life. He tried not to disturb Will but involuntary moans betrayed his own pain.

At first light Will staggered to his feet. He leant against the trunk of a gum tree until the world stopped spinning. He didn't have the energy to boil a billy, but poured cold water from his pannikin. He offered some to Nugget, who took a couple of laps.

'It's now or never Nug. I reckon I can just about stagger into town. Comin?'

The old dog raised his head. His tail signalled that he was willing but, try as he might, he could not rise.

'OK mate. Don't stress ya'self. We'll sit a while. It's not important.'

Will sat down again, his back resting against the tree and Nugget dragged his body the short distance to once again rest his head on Will's outstretched legs.

''I've had a good run for me money, Nug, and you've been with me through the best and the worst of it.' He managed a low chuckle. 'Do ya' remember that time in Newcastle when I was so pissed I couldn't stand, for all the tea in China? There I was, in the middle of Lambton road an' you snappin' at anyone who tried t' move me. We stopped a lot of traffic that day, didn't we?'

They spent the hours, Will remembering, and Nugget acknowledging the memories with a feeble wag of his tail.

'We won't be much missed, Nug. It's a long time since I've been of any use around the sheds. I reckon those last few jobs were given out of charity.' Will paused to catch his breath then continued his train of thought. 'It's a funny thing, charity. It's another name for love ya' know, and that's the point, boy. Some can give, with love, an' others dole it out as charity, but I never asked for either.'

The dog whined, perhaps on agreement or perhaps because his body was in pain.

'Silly old bugger, you wouldn't know anythin' about charity. You've got more love in ya' little black body than all the charity in the world.'

Will sighed and a tear or two trickled down his weathered cheeks. His hand rested on the dog's head, sometimes patting, sometimes just for physical contact.

They sat there all through the day, sometimes sleeping, sometimes just breathing, waiting for the last great tramp.

Nobody knew which went first but, when their bodies were found, it was clear that they had journeyed together to the end.

Aileen Pluker

Cape Barren Geese

Prison farm
Stately grey gleaners
follow the harvest
stand among sheep
picking segments of life
left by the reapers.

Low lines of stubble
lead geese to lake havens –
reflections
total fire of sunsets
out of reach
concealed from men behind walls.

Wings whisper power
decision.
Soft - the shadows fly
at dusk and autumn.
Seasons of geese
of men
ruled
by choices.

Helen van Rooijen

Archie

Archie was no oil painting.

Instead of having the sleek, white feathers of the Australian sulphur-crested cockatoo, Archie was bald, looking more like a diminutive substitute for the Christmas table.

I found him as a fledgling, cold and near death at the base of a large gum. He had either fallen or been pushed from the nest above. Despite all my family's forecasts of his imminent demise, Archie survived, and thrived, if one overlooked the unfortunate habit of his feather pulling.

Whenever feathers appeared he would either snap them off or pull them out. The exception was his crest which, compared with the rest of him, looked quite magnificent when he decided to display it. It was usually accompanied by an ear-splitting squawk and a cheeky, who's a pretty boy.

Many visits to the vet didn't solve the problem. His diet was changed many times to no avail. His cage had no door which allowed him free run of the house and yards, and boredom didn't seem to be the problem either. Archie was on good terms with nearly all the domestic animals around the farm, the shed cats, the sheep dogs and especially the chooks which he bossed unmercifully.

The exception to all this good will was Sweetie, a vicious, ill-tempered budgerigar belonging to my mother. All the family, especially Archie, were targets for this nasty, little bird's bloodletting. Ears were his favourite target. It wasn't unusual to see one or more of us walking around holding bloodied hankies after one of his attacks.

Sweetie was not nice and, except for my mother, we were all secretly pleased when one day he... mysteriously... disappeared.

Archie had a charmed life. The number of times he stripped electrical wires and wasn't fried could only be seen as a miracle. His closest call, however, came from my father.

Dad's pride and joy was a classic Mini Cooper S. He had spent nearly two years bringing the car back to factory condition. Archie spent two happy hours reducing it back to the pre-restoration state.

We heard Dad yelling outside and the fact that you would have heard him a couple of paddocks away, I knew he was angry. The shotgun in his hand wasn't a good sign either. He was standing by the side of the Mini when we got outside, no longer shouting. He seemed to be struck dumb as more and more damage became apparent.

The interior lining hung down in ribbons, and the new seat coverings with stuffing pulled out and scattered throughout the car had certainly provided entertainment for Archie. The outside hadn't fared any better. The chrome trim had been pulled out and bent, windscreen washers pulled off and under the bonnet, spark plug wires, distributor, thermostat and battery leads were all tangled together in an unrecognisable mess.

The situation, even at this stage, may have been diffused if only Archie had remained hidden. Of course he didn't. He came out from behind the front tyre, nipped the cap off the tyre valve and pushed down, letting the air escape. He then, with an impudent look at my father, put his head on the side and said who's a pretty boy.

43

For my father this was one, who's a pretty boy, too many.
He lifted the shotgun and fired.

He missed Archie but the Mini received both barrels.

Kathy Blacker

Sisterly Love

My smart little Grace
has a darling face
with eyes all lined in cream

Her sister however
has much more space
that place of her ears in between

She'll harass all the rest
be right on their case
yet to be chased herself makes her scream

Mary Gudzenovs

Wolves, Dogs and Genes

I owned a black Labrador for a few years prior to being married and six since, including our current girl, or middle-aged lady actually.

They are loyal, affectionate, gentle, good with children and excellent watchdogs who bark but rarely bite. I had always assumed that they protected our property but a friend told us one of our dogs only barked when we were home, not while we were out – interesting.

I had to learn with my first dog. We had been alerted by his breeder to the insatiable appetites of these dogs and fat Labs were part of the landscape. One used to visit the local butcher when the meat was delivered and of course his cuteness was well rewarded by the drivers.

I was keen to learn about the breed. They were named after the Canadian province as were Newfoundlands from next door. Trivia of the week is that the two provinces, are now one, called Labrador-Newfoundland. Both breeds were, and still are, on fishing boats to retrieve net ropes or items of gear that fell overboard and for land and sea rescues in these cold and foreboding waters and landscapes. They are close relatives genetically and geographically except Newfoundlands had a Mastiff get into the gene pool somewhere hence their huge size.

When I was first aware of their appetite I thought it was a great thing considering the icy world they live in. Woodcutteres in Canada are said to eat 10,000 calories a day in the winter whereas outdoor workers in temperate Australia need 2-3000 calories daily. Their appetites matched the dogs' environment, a win-win situation for man and dog assuming food was available.

That appetite satiated in Australian suburbia would almost certainly result in a fat and unhealthy dog unless it has a huge amount of exercise. I am pleased to say that it is not a lack of will power and moral fibre in our beloved Labradors. It is genes.

In the USA a year or so ago 300 Labradors' genetics were screened. Over 80% lacked what they called the 'Satiation gene.' This was a gene that essentially told the stomach to tell the brain 'Hey I am full now tell me to stop eating.' So the owner must take the place of that gene. That is hard because they look so pitiful when they want something.

They just will not listen to a rational discussion about diet and their health. It gets no traction whatsoever. Not much different to smokers I suppose.

Recently I saw a show, *Dog Tales*, on TV. It was about the relationship between man and dog that was described as the most successful cross species relationship in the animal kingdom. I just had a piece of cheese. My Lab's nose was a foot from my typing elbow. I turned to look at her and she wagged her tail. As soon as she saw there was no cheese left she shot off to see if Mum was a better shot.

Back to the point. All dogs come from wolves. There were three lots of data presented on *Dog Tales*. From archeological digs 10,000 years old were wolf skulls identical to today. There were also other canine skulls that were not wolves and not like each other.

Then there was an experiment in Russia on a farm where there were hundreds of wild foxes, bred for furs I assume. Their genetics are closest to wolves. They selected the most aggressive males and females and mated them for ten generations and similarly the least aggressive. They did not show the savage group but the gentle ones turned out to be as cute and cuddly as a pet dog.

So we know that wolves lived with humans, but so did different canines. So with time there were physical changes and the last examples shows that breeding can change behaviour.

Wolves are smarter than dogs but are difficult to train if they don't want to do something. Someone, somewhere asked the brilliant question. 'We assume dogs cohabited with man for food but is it possible that they like being with man, ie a friend?' They experimented again with some dogs they had trained to go into a MRI chamber. These dogs had been shown a red non-descript toy and patted, loved etc. The second lot of dogs had been shown a different toy that was yellow and then given food.

The brain response was measured by MRI. The dog that was fed had a response in the feeding section of the brain that looked to be maybe 1.5 x 1cm. The one that was NOT fed but loved had a response throughout virtually the whole brain – it lit up! This was caused by oxytocin, serotonin and dopamine the 'loving, feel good' hormones.

Finally there was a discussion about a genetic condition that makes some people literally love everyone. It was suggested that a mutation to this gene in dogs, but not wolves, occurred about 10,000 years ago.

Actually people who have dogs know their dogs love them.

We just didn't know why.

Peter Morton

Fowl Sunday

'They can jolly well have it back again!' Lettice fumed.

The chicken she had bought the day before for Sunday lunch was off. Definitely off. Angrily she wrapped it in several layers of paper and thrust it into a plastic carry bag. She was NOT going to leave it in HER bin to stink until next Friday's rubbish collection. She would dump it in the bin outside THEIR shop on the way to church.

'Bother,' Lettice heard the bell as she strode towards the church. Well she would have to be a minute or two late. It couldn't be helped. A few more steps and she would reach the garbage bin outside the chicken shop, then she would drop the bag and be on her way.

'Like a ride, Lettice?'

Oh no! Why couldn't they have been early this morning, or just a few minutes later and she could have been rid of the chicken.

'Thank you.' Reluctantly she climbed into the back seat hoping they wouldn't notice anything amiss.

'Nice morning isn't it? Better than yesterday!'

'Yes.' There was a fly crawling over the parcel. It must have been there when she got into the car. No time to look for another bin outside the church. She would have to wait until after the service. She settled herself in the accustomed seat next to her great friend Kate. The fly seemed to have gone, thank goodness.

'What have you got in the bag Lettice?' Trust Kate to be curious. Well, she could tell Kate. No harm there.

She muttered, 'It's a bad chicken.' Lettice wrapped the plastic bag tighter and pushed it against the end of the pew.

'Going to have it blessed, are you? Or did you bring it along to confession?' Kate could hardly contain her mirth.

'I was going to dump it in the bin outside the shop where I bought it,' said Lettice savagely. 'Then before the bin, someone stopped to offer me a lift. I could hardly tell them what I was about to do and ask them to wait, so I had to bring it with me.'

'Perhaps it will repent after the sermon,' chuckled Kate. A couple with a small child had taken the pew behind and those in front were filling up. She was sure they could smell that chicken.

The organist played the introduction to the first hymn and Lettice opened her book and stood up, trying to ignore the parcel at the end of the seat. Another young family, mother, father, and two pre-schoolers came to sit in the pew immediately in front. Lettice closed her eyes tightly while she knelt for opening prayers. She knew those youngsters never sat still for a minute. One friendly look would have them over or under the set before she could say 'Amen'.

The congregation sat for the Bible readings. Lettice glancing sideways, noticed two flies cavorting about an arm's length from the plastic bag. One of the pre-schoolers had noticed them too and was standing on his seat attempting to catch them. They eluded him. Finally he made an energetic lunge which propelled him hallway over the back of the seat, arms outstretched, so that he almost landed on top of the parcel. Lettice caught him just before his hand reached the plastic and swiftly turned him about, handing him to his father who smiled an apology and took the child on his lap. Was that a snicker she heard from Kate?

When the sermon began the children ran for the toybox in

the corner at the back of the church. Lettice was able to give her attention to the priest until, on hearing the rustle of plastic, she realised the toddler from the pew behind was using the back of her seat to steady himself and reach for the parcel. She smiled bravely at him, trying to refocus his attention on herself and offering her own hand for him to grasp. The distraction was only momentary. Little fingers were clawing at the plastic in a determined effort to draw the bag closer. Firmly, she grasped his hands in her own, saying 'No' very softly. The two-year-old struggled free and reached for the bag again. She snatched it off the seat and sat holding it, ignoring the indignant wail which rose from behind.

For the remainder of the sermon, her attention was fixed on her lap from which she could detect a faint, unmistakable odour. During the ensuing prayers she knelt with the chicken on the floor in front of her, her frosty glare daring the children in front to touch it. At the passing of the Peace she tucked it under her left arm while offering her right to her neighbours. She dared not catch Kate's eye for fear of setting her giggling again and she was almost certain the couple in front twitched their noses as they shook her hand.

What would she do at Communion time? She could hardly take the wretched thing to the altar rail with her. Kate would have hysterics. A cautious glance fore and behind showed the pre-schoolers and the toddler preoccupied with their toys. Quickly she returned the parcel to its original position at the end of the pew and propped a couple of kneelers against it.

Returning from Communion she was relieved to see that the kneelers were undisturbed. Relief turned to dismay. A large blowfly was crawling along the top of the bag. She watched it disappear behind the kneeler. On her knees again she willed the queue of Communicants to move faster while noting a second blowfly had now joined the first. Shooing them away would only draw attention to the parcel.

The notices were interminable, and the final hymn, she saw as she turned the page, had eight long verses. She could really smell that bird now. The juices must have soaked right through the newspaper. One of the blowflies had got itself trapped in the bag. It accompanied the whole of the hymn with a full and persistent Bzzt Bzzt.

As the procession passed with agonising slowness up the aisle Lettice resolved to stay on her knees, eyes shut, until she could risk a dash for the side door. Bzzt bzzt bzzzt. That wretched blowie was still inside the bag. She risked a quick peek. Maybe now. There were only two women chatting and they were further up the aisle. She grasped the parcel in her right hand and leapt to her feet. Bzzt bzzt. One of the women took a step towards her as she strode up the aisle, but Lettice smiled a little desperately, not slackening her pace. 'See you later in the week. Must dash now.' Bzzt bzzzt.

Out the door and along the street she strode until she reached the bin outside the chicken shop. Bzzt bzzt. It disappeared into the depth of the red bin.

'Good riddance,' she said and set off home. Her key turned in the lock and Lettice gave a great sigh of relief just as the phone began to ring.

'Hullo.'

'Fe-fi-fo-fum. I smell a chicken starting to hum,' chanted Kate, her voice cracking as laughter overcame her.

'Not any more you can't. I got rid of it.'

'Only you,' gasped Kate. 'Only you would bring a bad chicken to church.'

'And the blowflies! Oh, what people must have thought,' said Lettice. And then she began to laugh.

Margaret Vivian

Pelican

I wish I were a bird
preferably a pelican

with eyes like beads of jet
and a hairstyle quite outrageous.
I'd strut and clack my beak
daring and courageous

and when I tired of that
I'd spread my wings and fly
and skim across the wave tops
then soar a mile high

there among the clouds
I'd play hide-n-seek all day
leaving little flurries of mist
to show I'd passed that way
I wish I were a bird
definitely a pelican

Kathy Blacker

You'd Never Think...

Looking at me, a grey-headed granny carrying a bit too much weight and far too many wrinkles, you'd never think I won a buckjumping competition once, would you? And only about thirteen at the time.

Well, strictly speaking it was only a bucking donkey. Actually only a trained bucking donkey. And I shared the honour – there was no prize – with my sister, a year younger than me. Still, it was a big donkey.

It happened like this.

A travelling show of rough-riders came to the small country town that was the centre of our district. Our farm was eleven miles out but this was the place we bought our stores, collected our mail, consigned our cream cans; the railway station where we trucked our wheat and wool and collected our super; and where we drove to see even rarer visiting live shows, like the blind violinist, or the small family circus that came once or twice. Or the rough-riders' show.

It was set up on the common, where the townspeople ran their milking cows and buggy horses among the scattered gums. When we arrived they'd built a circular arena with high railed sides, put up tiers of plank seats around it, and run a tall canvas wall outside the lot, to prevent anyone watching the show for nothing. That canvas kept out the wind too, because it was a cold night. I remember my sister and I were wearing jumpers and pleated plaid skirts, all made by our mum.

There were a couple of lorries and a caravan or two parked outside, and lights strung here and there. The show much have brought its own generator; our town had no electricity supply then. Under these unfamiliar lights Dad bought our tickets and we trooped inside.

We picked seats halfway up one of the tiers. There were yards of empty planking to choose from. Our district was not closely settled in those days and we couldn't have mustered the numbers to fill the seats if we had rounded up every man, woman and child from every house in the town and every distant farm.

I suppose the men who rode the horses were comparatively young men, but then they looked middle-aged to me, and the leathery owner, who was also ringmaster appeared positively geriatric. And I can't remember a great deal about the bucking displays, only being alarmed once that a rearing horse would fall backwards on its rider and crush him against the rails. Then the ringmaster turned this large grey donkey, wearing no saddle or bridle, into the ring and invited the young men and youths of the district to see if they could ride it.

At that time my sister and I had just about given up saddles. Usually we were cowboys as we acted out the stories we invented, but about then we'd switched to Red Indians and rode bareback for miles as the braves raided all over the farm. So, after we had watched the boys tumbling, first one by one and then two at a time, over the donkey's head we asked Dad if we could have a go.

He must have been confident we could do it, or else that we couldn't come to much harm if we were thrown off, because our dad, that most protective man, said yes. Surprised and gratified, down we jumped from plank to plank and waited outside the rails.

As the kids say today, in the end it was no big deal. That donkey had been carefully trained to give three bucking heaves to throw his rider on to his neck, whereupon he would lower his head and the hapless rider, with nothing to grab, would roll down the incline to the dust.

I can't remember whether my sister or I had first ride, but the wily old donkey didn't even bother to lower his head. If after three heaves the rider was safely behind his withers he just stopped, and stood with his ears dropping looking bored until whoever it was dismounted and the next rider got on. My sister stuck on until he stopped, I stuck on, we stayed on him both together. Another girl we knew stayed on him too, but when she rode double her co-rider must have pushed her off, for the ringmaster said the two sisters were the winners.

So there you are. My moment of glory, when my sister and I rode the bucking donkey and beat the boys of the district and some of the young men as well – all of them older then we were, anyway. I only wish now I'd been old enough myself to relish their discomfiture as well as my own triumph.

They were chauvinists to a man, I discovered as I grew up.

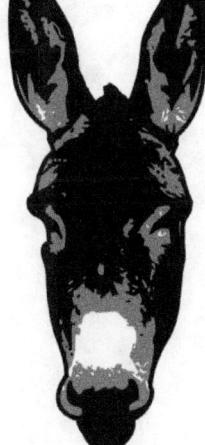

Alison Manthorpe

A Butterfly Blessing

I sat, mourning for my loss,
You came, resting gently on my hand,
   blessed and consoled me,
Your life, measured in moments,
   not in days
yet you found time to come,
to decorate my hand with fragile wings,
delicate as the finest lace,
reminding me there is beauty
even in the darkest place.

Aileen Pluker

The Squadron

The squadron splits up to make separate approaches to the landing site.

A humming, growing steadily louder is the first indication of the attack.

The squadron leader spots a likely landing place and begins the descent followed by several of his band; a quick but skilled landing, the job accomplished and off again before the enemy can retaliate.

Several more runs and the enemy is decidedly restless.

The squadron leader heads in for the final attack, but just prior to landing he is dealt a crippling blow, catapults sideways, and spins out of control.

The rest of the squadron beats a hasty retreat, watching helplessly as their comrade crashes into the pile of dirty laundry beside the bed.

The enemy rubs its balding head and rolls over.

'Bloody mosquitoes.'

Mary Gudzenovs

Fishy Fish

I wonder where that fish did go
Too deep for me to ever know
That scheming, cheeky, sodding thing
Keeps pinching bait from off my string!

I've tried before to bag that fish
To make a tasty breakfast dish
It knows I'm after it for sure
But gulps the bait, then grabs for more!

I'm sick of serving tea down there
For you to steal without a care
So just you wait, you wretched fish
One day you'll get your deathly wish!

Adrian McFarlane

Jonathan Livingston Friesian

It was an unusually warm, autumn day in County Clare and Michael O'Sullivan's identical big, white Friesian dairy cows, who had spent their day going about their daily business of eating green grass to fill their huge udders with lovely, creamy milk had just left the dairy. On the walk back to the paddock they felt lighter in spirit and udderwise.

They were philosophical, social creatures and discussed weighty matters such as their calves and the ginormous, stud bull Longfellow that they had glimpsed in a big truck being unloaded into the shed a few days ago.

That was as close as they would get to the big fella, as he was the father to many of them, including Lizzie Longfellow, who was regarded as Big Mamma or Boss Cow.

No-one, except perhaps Lizzie, thought that this would be an important day in the world of cows.

She was leading as usual and not joining in the usual chatter. She felt strange. She blinked her eyes, looked around at her friends, at the sheep in a nearby paddock, at a nuisance rabbit that nearly got in her way. All the while she chewed and chewed her cud.

She stopped suddenly and turned around to her friends. 'Sorry I have been so grumpy. I know now what has been upsetting me. We need to talk.'

They mooed their assent but some turned to their friends mooing, 'not another lecture' or 'this could be interesting' but they all stopped, nibbled grass and settled down.

Lizzy mooed softly, 'Girls, ladies, fellow bovines, have you ever realised we do the same thing day in, day out, eat, make milk. We have our calves at the same time and they are taken at the same time too.'

Lizzie waited for a reply, then continued. 'We are all the same size, shape, height and weight and we all have the same white colour. But I heard recently that one Friesian cow, by name, Colleen, from a field in Athenry, jumped over the moon.'

A few stopped chewing their cud in mid chew but soon began again.

'Wouldn't ye be wanting to do something like that?'

They looked at her, dumbfounded.

Fat Lips mooed, 'Like what?'

'Well, we could pull carts, pretend to be bulls, dig holes in the ground.' They did not seem interested.

'Why don't you suggest something Fat Lips. After all you're the stupid cow who asked the bull to kiss you.'

'Well, I learned my lesson,' Fat Lips replied. She hated her name.

There was a mooing of agreement. Though cattle are followers none of them would follow Lizzie. They didn't want a life of fun, excitement, adventure. They just wanted to be cows.

Fat Lips explained, 'Lizzie, it's not such a bad life, being a dairy cow. Plenty of food and water, giving milk twice a day, a date with a bull once a year. Isn't that enough? Pleasant company, good food and a nice place to live.'

Lizzie was hurt. No-one understood. Not one of them wished to change their nature. She could no longer be their leader. That day she walked among the others, ruminating in her stomach, as cows do, but she also ruminated in her mind. She thought of her friends as 'dumb German Holsteins', a very insulting term in Ireland. They would never understand.

At the start of the very cold winter she noticed that the ponds in the paddock were freezing over. She remembered her mother saying that when this happens they would have to lick the ice but be very careful not to walk on it for fear of falling in.

But one day some teenage girls and boys came into the paddock, dressed in caps and colourful clothes and began sliding over the water. They turned, twisted and glided over the ice just like people she had seen on the TV in the dairy.

This is it, she thought. This is what she would do to be different.

After milking that night, by the light of the silvery moon, she tippy toed onto the ice. She started a slippery walk, but soon began gliding side to side as she had seen it done on TV. She wriggled her backside as she followed the border of the frozen pond.

She had always been a heavy cow but now she felt as light as a rabbit running around a paddock. She relaxed, then remembered seeing someone lifting one leg on the ice. She could do that, after all she had three more.

She lifted one back leg and pushed it to the side, losing her balance and crashing through the ice.

Some of the cows had been watching and when she struggled up the bank they mooed their laughter. It was a very muddy pond and she was covered in black muddy spots.

They can laugh, she thought, but I like them. They make me different.

She began swimming regularly, each time coming out the

with different markings.

Bovine and Bovina, the God and Goddess of cows saw this and liked it. Lizzie looked much grander with black markings on a white background. It made her different from the herd. So they decreed that every Friesian should be born with different spots. And that is why each Friesian calf is born with black markings and they keep their individual pattern of black and white markings for all of their lives.

Peter Morton

Cat

So you think that you have tamed me?
Cured me of my predatory ways?
Won my allegiance with your kindness?
I have news for you, my friend.

I might sit upon your lap and purr
Permit you to buy me food
And you think this means you own me?
You have never been so wrong.

Watch me when I hear a rustle
Or a twitter in a bush
See me flatten out and slowly, softly
Slink toward unsuspecting prey.

I come so close but they don't see me
With one quick, agile leap I pounce
My claws, unsheathed are sharp and deadly
I execute with speed and grace.

I can twist through narrow spaces.
Leap from heights and land upright.
The world's most effective hunter.
I can survive all by myself.

I will accept your praise and petting.
I'll pander to your every need.
But please remember I'm a cat and
I will do just as I please.

Aileen Pluker

The Message

Candles flickered. The diamond pane windows clattered shut on a violent gust.

Derida sat up, still fully dressed and now wide-awake. The hardback slipped from the covers, landing on the floor with a heavy thump.

Her senses told her that whatever had woken her, it wasn't the slamming of the windows... and it had come from elsewhere in the house.

Maybe it was the cat. Simeon, had been frustratingly obnoxious since the Mallory's from next door had gone on holiday, taking their tortoiseshell Annabelle, with them. He had been over there every day to check. Anybody would think he was suffering a broken heart, Derida huffed, climbing off the bed.

But there was a possibility it was a burglar. She reached down behind the headboard and retrieved the foot long barbecue kebab steel. Just in case.

Slipping the leather thong securely over her wrist she brandished it as she ventured into the short corridor, past the front door and into the lounge. Even in the dark she could tell it was empty.

Derida's boyfiiend, Adam, was always telling her she should get a burglar alarm. Living eight miles out of town gave her all the peace and tranquillity she needed for her painting, but it also left her vulnerable.

The Mallory's homestead was a fifteen-minute walk away and Derida's was the last house on the dirt road. Beyond, open farmland stretched as far as the eye could see.

Adam's dire predictions preyed heavily on her mind as she crept toward the kitchen.

A noise stopped her in her tracks.

She lowered the steel and with one hand propped on her hip strode into the kitchen and flipped the light switch.

'Bad cat!' she scolded Simeon, who was hurriedly placing himself out of reach on top of the eight foot pantry.

'Yow,' he replied.

'Don't 'yow' at me you little horror!' Derida snapped, surveying the mess on the timber tabletop.

The watercolour she had left to dry beside its subject – a vase of roses – lay ruined in the midst of a puddle of water. Simeon loved flowers. He would sit in the garden and bat at them playfully, sniffing the fallen petals with rapture. But this was the first time he had attacked a vase of cut blooms.

Derida grouched at the cat as she mopped up the water and swept both roses and painting into the bin. Simeon sat tall, secure in the knowledge that she would not climb up to get him. She was scared of heights, which he had soon discovered was to his advantage. His bright green eyes seemed to sparkle with amusement. Derida noticed.

'Well, I don't think it's funny young man. No treats for you till you start behaving properly.'

Simeon dropped into a sphinx pose and yowled, looking less triumphant.

'No point apologising now. You've done your dash.'

She left the kitchen in a huff; leaving him in the dark. Seconds later she heard thuds as Simeon landed on the table and then the floor. He caught up as she reached the bedroom and darted in before she could object. He waited on the bed.

Derida ignored him, blowing out the remaining floating candle, undressing and climbing under the covers. Simeon's black tail drooped. He stood watching as she snuggled down. He moved to settle beside his mistress but she pushed him off the bed and wagged a finger in front of his nose.

'No, you're in disgrace. You can sleep in your own basket.'

The next time she woke it was 5.30 and light outside. The wind had picked up and was moaning through the trees surrounding the house.

She lay in the comfort of her bed considering her options. She could snuggle down and try to go back to sleep, or, she could get up, have breakfast and do the dishes she had been trying to ignore for the last two days.

A sound from the kitchen made up her mind. Damn cat!

Shrugging into her housecoat, Derida hurried down the corridor. Her eyes took a moment to adjust to the fluoro, then she could see Simeon. He was in his favourite spot on top of the pantry. Every hair on end!

'Simmie, what's wrong?' she cried, alarmed by his display.

Still moving she failed to notice the back door to her left, open just a crack, and the figure that moved in behind her.

Simeon hissed savagely, crouching low.

Derida felt the hand on her shoulder and realised too late that the barbecue steel was still propped against the sink on the other side of the kitchen.

Pulled around to face her attacker, Derida screamed when a knife flashed close to her face. She didn't even hear his first demand for her money. A backhanded slap cleared her hearing but also sent her stumbling against the table and onto the floor.

'Where's your money?' he yelled again.

'I don't keep any in the house,' she lied through her tears.

He lifted a hand to hit her again and she cringed.

Simeon decided enough was enough. He came down from the pantry in a streak of black fur and claws, landing on the back of the intruder's neck.

Surprised by the sudden attack he dropped the knife and tried to grab the scratching, hissing ball.

Derida took a few seconds to gather her wits. Then she kicked at the knife. It skittered across the floor and disappeared beneath the stove. She planted her feet against the intruders' chest and pushed. He sat down hard and Simeon leapt to the floor.

Stunned by the sudden two pronged attack the intruder sat swearing colourfully and wiping at blood that trickled from his hands, neck and ears.

Meanwhile, Derida crawled under the table and was halfway down the corridor before he could get to his feet.'

The bedroom door was heavy and so was the chair that she pushed against it.

'I'm calling the police!' she screamed, digging frantically in her shoulder bag.

He was rattling the doorknob and banging against the door.

'I cut the lines sweetheart!' he gloated.

'Well, there's not much you can do about a mobile MATE!' she yelled back, punching in 000.

Simeon was standing, puffed and stiff legged in the middle of the bed, hissing at the closed door.

The police told her to barricade herself in till they could get there, so as soon as she hung up Derida put her shoulder to the wardrobe and pushed it across the window.

There were no sounds from the corridor now. Simeon had stopped hissing and was simply sitting, watching his mistress pace up and down. She took that as a good sign.

By the time the police arrived Simeon was washing his paws nonchalantly. At the sound of the cars he pricked up his ears, twitched his nose and yowed.

The police found the intruder at the Mallory's, tending his wounds, and arrested him without incident. He had made himself at home and apparently had been there a few days.

Once the police had taken their statement and notified Adam for her, Derida was left alone to wait for her boyfriend. She hopped in the shower to freshen up and as she was dressing Simeon sat and watched contentedly, eyes half closed.

Derida picked up the cat and cradled him like a baby.

'Is that the message you were trying to convey with your behaviour? That there was someone over there that shouldn't have been?'

'Yow,' he said, patting her nose tentatively with a paw.

'If you hadn't distracted him when you did things might not have turned out so good.' She scratched him affectionately between the ears. 'And you're forgiven for ruining that painting. Full treat rights have been restored.'

Simeon closed his eyes and purred luxuriously.

Mary Gudzenovs

Night Song

'Pretty me Pretty me'
a willy wagtail sat
on the western full moon
and sang its territory.

'Pity me Pity me'
sang to the bracelet of stars
flung across the sky – but
when the moon was lost
he sulked his head and slept

and so did I.

Helen van Rooijen

A Game of Snakes and Mother

My mother, who we called Mim, was a country woman. She'd been raised in the outback by her father who had followed the shearing circuit round southern Queensland and north western NSW. She was tougher than anyone I've ever known.

Her real name was Mimmette and she hated it. Everybody, including we five kids, had to call her Mim because she said no-one should have too many fancy titles; they were a waste of time.

Dad met Mim during the floods of '56 out in the channel country, and it was literally love at first sight. She was lifting ewes onto the back of her ute trying to evacuate a flooding paddock. He'd never seen such a good worker, let alone a woman who could lift a fully grown sheep off the ground and put it in a truck. She was what he referred to as a good sort; pretty as a field of hay bales and more useful than a kelpie-bluey cross.

Mim was an extraordinary mother. Some of what she knew about motherhood and being a wife she learnt from the *Womans Day*. The rest she worked out by watching the station animals and from listening to *Blue Hills* on the radio. Dad looked after the animals and machinery. Mim did the rest.

During childhood I saw my mother cope with more crises than any TV series could dream up. But, to her, a bushfire approaching the house or an infestation of rats in the pantry was something 'that the Good Lord had sanctioned, otherwise it wouldn'ta happened'. She simply rolled up the sleeves, organised us to do our bit, and got on with it.

Looking back now I realise that while helping deliver a

twisted calf from a lurching bush cow was all in a day's work for Mim, some of her actions and attitudes were not only stoic but downright heroic. And she was funny, probably because she wasn't trying. Besides that, to her, trying to be funny was a waste of energy when pigs needed slopping and firewood needed cutting.

My mother had a secret recipe for country fricassee. She prepared it at random times throughout summer and insisted we all eat it 'cause it was fancy and she didn't do fancy if she didn't have to'. Country fricassee was chewy and tasted something like chicken, but since none of the farm's chickens ever seemed to be missing and trips to the Hill for supplies were rare events, I always suspected that other ingredients were involved.

She also hated snakes, particularly those of the brown variety. She told us to chase them with a stick and if we could, to stove in their heads with a shovel or whatever was handy.

'Sneaky little buggers. Into everything and they'd kill ya if ya didn't get them first,' she'd say, as if it was normal to knock one of the deadliest creatures on earth on the head.

Mim kept a loaded shotgun in the kitchen and outside just near the woodpile. One day we were doing our lessons in the schoolroom when we heard an enormous crack followed by a small explosion just outside the house. As we charged out to see what all the fuss was about we heard Mim screaming.

'Ya rotten little buggers. Look what ya done to the boiler!' Her face was red with anger and the shotgun hung loosely from her hands.

It turned out that our new boiler, the one that took Grayson's Department Store a full six months to get in for Dad, the one which had cut down Mim's fetching and carrying by half, the one Mim prized above her best crockery, was dead.

She'd seen the little bugger's head pop out from under the tank stand. As she'd fetched the shotgun the snake had slithered behind the fibro protector around the boiler stand. Unfortunately, the little bugger was too quick for Mim's usual deft shooting. She tried to follow its path but when both barrels exploded with the full force of a country woman's anger the boiler exploded as the two shells pierced its precious casing.

We were mortified. We now had to cut and carry more wood than ever. Baths were less regular and the new boiler did take another six months to order and deliver from Sydney.

Mim shrugged it off. Said, 'You kids were gettin' too soft. Won't hurt ya to miss out on luxuries. Pity about the snake.'

Another time, when 'the brownies were everywhere', we were having a picnic down by the creek. It was a rare treat but it was so hot even Mim conceded that work was out of the question. We had driven in the ute to the lone creek which wound its way through our property. Mim had prepared mutton sandwiches and Dad had set up the campfire to boil the billy. Just as we began to sip on our sweet black tea Mim suddenly lifted herself off the log and declared, 'Dad, quick, the keys. The little buggers are everywhere.'

Before we had time to know what all that meant, Mim was in the ute tearing through the creekbed to the dry grass flat on the other side. She drove madly about the space completing the tightest figure of eights imaginable. Then she would suddenly scream to a dusty halt and reverse madly back over the track she'd just covered. All the while, we climbed up on the lower branches of the coolabah near our picnic so we could see what was going on.

'It's the brownies I reckon,' said Dad laconically. 'You know how much she hates them.' Meanwhile the rodeo continued. Mim drove like a madwoman testing every bolt and bit in that old car as she chased down the enemy. We could hear random shouts of 'Yippee', and 'Got ya'.

When Mim finally stopped in a haze of red dust we bolted over to see what the show had been all about. We saw the squished bodies of dozens of brown snakes ghoulishly laid out among the dry grass and tyre tracks all over the flat.

'Here kids. Take this and get the good bits before they go off,' Mim ordered and smiled one of her rare smiles. We took the hessian bag and collected what body parts weren't too mangled or flat. And for the next week we ate country fricassee. And no chicken seemed to have died in the making of that week's menu.

Mim had a soft spot for crows. She liked their shiny black feathers and intelligent bearings. 'Pretty little buggers, aren't they?' I heard her tell Dad one day. I don't think he agreed as he looked down at his boots and shuffled a bit. Dad had learnt to agree and not to disagree. He told me when I was fourteen that that's how a man keeps the good ones. I wouldn't disagree, even now.

Mim liked crows until she decided to try her hand at growing a garden.

'Sick of all the canned stuff, the dried stuff, the stuff with the weevils,' she said.

She got us to work on her patch. It really was only a patch. Four rows of raised dirt. She planted corn and 'tatas', some lettuce and 'matoes'. We watered them every morning and night with a bucket from one of the horse troughs under the station windmill.

'Precious water,' she'd say sagely, 'Don't spill any. Bet the fricassee will be even better with fresh veggies.' And miraculously, Mim's little garden flourished and the corn and the lettuce and the potatoes and tomatoes grew into a respectable, unexpected garden of Eden.

She was so proud. The scarecrows she'd built from rusty farm machinery and handed-down, hand-me-down kids clothes looked proud. Even the crows looked down proudly as they sat on the arm of the whirling windmill.

For some reason, sparrows, starlings, magpies and even rabbits stayed way. Perhaps they knew Mim's reputation with a shotgun. Perhaps snakes gossip.

Mim somehow trusted those crows until the corn started to disappear and the tomatoes were decorated with holes and their luscious red centres were left drying and brown in the hot summer sun.

Mim was sure it was maggies and so she set a trap. She hung two rows of washing, mostly sheets needing a scrub, along a line discreetly placed not far from the garden. After the morning jobs were complete she'd station herself between the two rows of sheets. It was a tedious job because it was always hot and she didn't really know when the culprits would turn up. After two days of watching through the gaps in the sheets she abandoned her post and declared, 'They won't be back. They must have heard I wasn't happy.'

I reckon they must have seen her boots under the sheet as

she'd been sitting on her box waiting to spring the thieves. The view from the windmill would have been perfect and crows are cunning, patient creatures. As soon as the sentry abandoned her post, they swooped and did their best to spoil Mim's delight.

The day after the raid she found black feathers, long glossy black feathers in the garden. 'Aint maggies or the parrots,' she declared oblivious to the squadron of black fiends awaiting their next raid.

But, the crows who had been so clever at avoiding human intervention didn't reckon on my little sister Martha's unexpected trip to the toilet. The morning after another strange fricassee we had all been feeling queasy but Martha had scored more runs than Bradman this particular day. She left Mim with the rest of us in the schoolhouse as we strained unenthusiastically through the correspondence lessons of the day.

Martha suddenly turned up in the schoolhouse. 'Mimmy, come quickly, the cwows are eating the fwood.' Rushing outside, Mim saw that her trusted feathered friends were in fact the dreaded enemy.

With rage, normally only reserved for brown snakes, Mim swooped on the shotgun and sprayed the garden area with bullets. Black feathers filled the air, and two fortunate crows squawked loudly as they headed for the open sky.

The garden scheme was over and we returned to our regular veggie diet of the canned stuff, the dried stuff, and the stuff with the weevils. Crows were rarely seen on the windmill after that, or in the district for that matter.

Our country fricassee had more variety too; not quite as

much like chicken all the time. The meat was always a little more sinewy and occasionally a black feather or two would make it less palatable.

Mim raised us tough. She made sure we were clothed and fed well enough. And she made sure we never expected more from life than we were prepared to put in. Despite her matter of fact ways and her irrational hatred of some native species she did love us and our dad. And she always made us smile, even though we made sure she never knew it was happening.

Ross Hudson

DOLPHINS
– Morning and Night

Morning
Last night the sea slept well, dreamless,
bed linen barely ruffled.
In dawn's silver silky light
the first ripples drift when tides
begin to stir.
The wind yawns
and plays kissing games
with a lone dolphin, now rolling slow
hissing troughs tugging V's on satin sheets.

Night
Dolphins as silver needles stitch the fraying threads
Of creaming bow waves
tack patches and drifts of biting cold spray
white caps arch purple colour-slip green wake
and merge bluster cloud to endless sky
then
dolphins ride before our keel
and safely sew the sea-seams to home.

Helen van Rooijen

Beginnings

From the top of the hill my shadow
attenuated
angular as a stick insect
sways over grass tipped with sunlight
like fur.

A grave behind me
unmarked, long forgotten,
holds bones of an old pony
forty or thereabouts when he died.

He carried more children than anyone bothered to count
passing from sister to brother
from farm to farm
whenever the heels that drummed on his shaggy ribs
reached too low.
And all those children are grandparents now.
Or gone after him.

But I can remember his mane under my hand
how he smelled in the rain
how my world of five years
changed suddenly
splendidly
viewed from his back.

Only two of us know where he lies.
We were the last.
The sister who shared the pony
remembers the bits I forget.

Alison Manthorpe

The Brick Factory

The first I knew anything was wrong was when I saw Ethel's nose. That pristine muzzle, normally such a stark contrast to her gleaming black coat, was on this morning smudged in a sticky grime and coated with bits of leaf and grain.

She stood at the gate with the others, feigning innocence and trying not to look me in the eye. But that nose was the give-away, and when I leaned across the fence, I smelled the final incriminating evidence – molasses. The donkeys had broken into the hay shed again.

As I hurried toward the nearby building I did a quick mental stock-take of an it contained. Still hoping my little darlings had simply managed to pull the four gallon jug through the dividing wall, I halted in the door to survey the damage.

All six bales of meadow hay lay ruptured and scattered about the floor. The three grain bins – two that had held chaff and one Stable Mate – lay crushed and empty in various corners. Bound by the molasses and mixed by sixteen milling hooves, the entire contents of my shed lay trampled into a sort of bizarre muesli from which, it was safe to assume, the donkeys had eaten their fill. But there was one item housed in the shed I'd forgotten about.

Panic seized me as I picked up the torn husk of a plastic-lined paper bag. Somewhere mixed into this donkey banquet were twenty kilos of construction cement. The fine powder, like a dusting of sugar over their strong-tasting breakfast, would have gone down completely unnoticed by my greedy herd.

What would it do to their stomachs, I wondered as I

staggered numbly from the shed. Surely their delicate equine digestive tracts couldn't cope with such a powerful irritant. Colic, it appeared, was going to be the least of our problems.

As I passed the four guilty parties in the yard I gave them each a hug. What good were reprisals now – my babies would all be dead by morning.

My husband, who has never shared my love of animals and is continually looking for donkey meat recipes in all our cookbooks, greeted this news with great delight. Never again would he be awakened by raucous braying at six a.m. on a Saturday morning, or have to share a bottle of his home-brewed stout with Clancy, our resident alcoholic.

Fortunately for the rest of us, the disaster I'd envisaged did not come to pass. The following morning, aside from a bit of industrial strength flatulence, my donks were all fit and well, if somewhat heavier.

Michael didn't miss out entirely though. He still enjoys telling his mates down the pub of the time his wife discovered a new and original way to make bricks.

Diane Hester

And Introducing

Eyre Writers Inc

Adrian McFarlane – A valued and missed member of Eyre Writers. He used the atmosphere of his home at the Tumby Bay caravan park to produce poetry and witty observances of human nature.

Aileen Pluker – Sometimes known as the Silver Fox. Was born in Melbourne but has been a West Coaster for fifty years. A member of Eyre Writers since 1990. Writes in a variety of genres: Plays, Young Adult, Crime and Historic Fiction.

Alison Manthorpe grew up on a farm, worked as a physio, married a master mariner, accompanied him to sea in yachts. Retired to Coffin Bay and now to Adelaide. Long-term bookbug fascinated by words. Awarded for short stories and poetry. Published poet.

Diane Hester's debut thriller, Run To Me, was published by Random House Australia and short-listed in the U.S. Daphne du Maurier Awards for Excellence in Mystery/Suspense. Born in New York, Diane came to Australia in 1978 as a violinist with the Adelaide Symphony.

Helen van Rooijen – A retired social worker who has been writing and reading all her life. Winner of short story and poetry prizes and has had a short film made of one story. Has published a series of three detective thrillers and currently working on a new character and story to publish in 2021.

Kathy Blacker – Former nurse, travelled extensively as an airhostess, had great fun working as a radio announcer, copy-writer, and program producer, and so far has two unpublished novels under her belt.

Lee Clayton – Ex-policeman and government employee. Worked in New Guinea and Queensland with indigenous peoples and writes about those experiences, the effects of war, and the underestimated value of women in history.

Margaret Vivian – Retired music teacher and past writer of short stories, poetry and articles. Valued Life Member of Eyre Writers.

Mary Gudzenovs – Historian, novelist and short story writer with a passion for animals and the weird and wonderful world around us.

Peter Morton – Born and educated in Adelaide and spent almost 50 years as a Rural Doctor. Has had 30 magazine articles, and four books about his life and the stories of many others who have lived, worked, and succeeded in the "bush" published.

Ross Hudson – Retired farmer from Tumby Bay, passionate about local history and family. Writes historical faction about South Australia and its people.

VK Tritschler – A Kiwiadian who moved to Australia and found the support of this writing group who helped make her an author. She now has several published books and surrounds herself with family, friends and a menagerie of animals. To read her latest book check out **www.vktritschler.com**